For Billy, who has been waiting
J. E. M.

For T. N. H.
S. G.

First edition 2010

Library of Congress Cataloging-in-Publication Data

Macken, JoAnn Early, date.
Waiting out the storm / JoAnn Early Macken ; illustrated by Susan Gaber.—1st ed.
p.   cm.
Summary: A mother reassures her child about the wind, lightning,
and thunder when a storm passes through.
ISBN 978-0-7636-3378-3
[1. Stories in rhyme. 2. Storms—Fiction. 3. Rain and rainfall—Fiction.
4. Mother and child—Fiction.]
I. Gaber, Susan, ill. II. Title.
PZ8.3.M187Wai 2010
[E]—dc22   2008030746

09 10 11 12 13 14 CCP 10 9 8 7 6 5 4 3 2 1

Printed in Shenzhen, Guangdong, China

This book was typeset in Calligraphic.
The illustrations were done in acrylic.

Candlewick Press
99 Dover Street
Somerville, Massachusetts 02144

visit us at www.candlewick.com

Waiting Out the Storm

JoAnn Early Macken ❧ illustrated by Susan Gaber

CANDLEWICK PRESS

Mama?

Yes, buttercup?

What's that I hear?

It's only the wind in the treetops, my dear.

Why does it whistle?

A storm's on its way.
The wind calls the raindrops
to come out and play.

They come when the wind calls?

They burst from the cloud,
skipping and leaping and laughing out loud.
They spin and they tumble. They bounce on the breeze.
They dance to the tune of the wind in the trees.

Mama?

Yes, buttercup?

What's that I hear?

That's just the rumble of thunder, my dear.

It's too loud! I'm afraid!

Oh, it's only a sound.
Thunder stomps. Thunder stumbles and bumbles around.

What is it doing?

It's racing up high,
chasing the lightning all over the sky.

But lightning's too tricky.
It starts and it stops.

It flashes and dashes between the raindrops.

What will the turtles do?

Oh, don't you fret.
Turtles like being outside when it's wet.

Like ducks?

Yes! Ducks paddle in water all day.
Puddles are ducks' favorite places to play.

What about chipmunks?

*They snuggle together,
deep in their burrows in wet, windy weather.*

And birds? Where do birds go?

Beneath Mama's wings.
When rains fall and winds blow,
the mama bird sings,

"Hush, little chickadees.
Never you fear.
There, there. You're safe now,
and I am right here."

We're comfy inside.

Yes, we'll stay dry and warm,
cozy together here out of the storm.

Tomorrow the sun will shine.
Then we'll go play.
We'll splash in the pond
like the ducks do all day.
But for now, let's just watch.
It's a wonder to see.
I am so glad I have you to share it with me.

So come, darling buttercup,
here where it's warm.
Like chickadee babies,
we're safe from the storm.
While winds blow and rains fall,
we'll wait out the weather.

Cozy as bunnies!

Yes, snuggling together.